Nancy Wi...

BRIGHT
NIGHT

THE STORY OF ANNE BRADSTREET

Illustrations by Louise Brewer

BRIGHT NIGHT

THE STORY OF ANNE BRADSTREET

ISBN# 1-930710-44-5
Copyright ©2000 Veritas Press

Veritas Press
1250 Belle Meade Drive
Lancaster, PA 17601

First edition

Nancy Wilson

BRIGHT
NIGHT

THE STORY OF ANNE BRADSTREET

Illustrations by Louise Brewer

To my little Jema.
—Nancy Wilson

To my Mother.
—Louise Brewer

Do you know Anne Bradstreet? She grew up in England long ago. She was slight as a garden wren but full of fun. Her house was big and grand and had many a shelf of shining books.

When she was a girl, she was taught to read, and she sought out tales of knights and gnomes, fights, flights, and frights. She sat on her papa's knee, and he would read into the night.

She was taught to knead bread to bake, and knit and spin with silk and wool. She would sigh when she caught sight of ink and pen, for Anne wrote fine rimes for men.

She caught smallpox and was ill a long time. She could not eat a crumb and was half-numb with fever. Yet Anne fought the blight till she was well.

She was wed to Simon Bradstreet when
she was sixteen years old. Anne and Simon
left England soon after and went on a ship to
a new land.

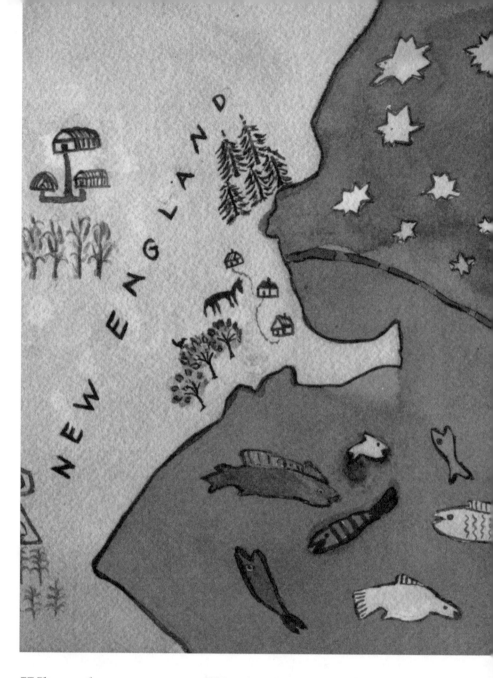

When the sea was still, the stars shone bright in the night sky, and Anne thought of her new home in New England. When the waves were high and the sea was harsh, the wild

wind did howl and storms did roar and rage. The ship did knock and wrench on the sea. Yet they did always trust God and pray for a safe landing.

One morning they stood on the deck and caught sight of land. The ship went straight for the shore. They were full of thanks that

they did not sink or wreck on the beach. With joy, Anne wrote home right away to tell of her brave sail.

There in the new land Anne had her children. She brought them up and taught them to love and praise God so that they might do no wrong, but only right as they

ought. Anne wrote about her children and her
life. She had a knack for writing sweet poems,
and it brought her much joy. Anne was known
to be a wise, meek, and good wife.

When Anne was old, her son did ask her to write for him all she knew of life and love and God. He knew this was more than all that could be bought with gold.

She wrote it all down for her son. Some in the town thought Anne should not write, but should only sew and spin.

Yet she sought to love God in all she wrote.
She wrote of yellow trees and swimming
lakes, of sky and cloud and wood and knoll.

In all she saw God's good hand: a calf, a wren, a gnat—all were His, and naught was too small for Him to reach.

One night Anne and Simon did smell
smoke. The sky was bright with puffs of
smoke that rose from the roof. The house was
in a wreath of flames. The night was bright
with the light of the fire.

The porch was black, the windows shook, the stair did break, the roof fell in. They did try with all their might to stop the fire, but it did burn all the night.

In the morning the house was no more. Anne saw all her nice things lost to the fire: her chest, her bed, her bench, her clock. She wrung her hands, she wept with sad sobs. They felt like wretches. Was this God's wrath?

No. Then did Simon and Anne kneel and thank God for their plight. They would not speculate about God's plan for them, for He would bless. They were dependent on His grace and would not let this loss hurt their faith.

The bright night was to them fraught with fright and loss. Yet, the night shone bright with the light of God's help and love and care. Anne and Simon knew God was good, and they did trust Him to show

His might and kindness to them.

Anne wrote a poem about the fire in her house and how God taught her to rest in His good gifts. She also wrote poems about her grandchildren.

Some of her newborn grandchildren got sick
and did die. It was sad to put the babes in
their graves. Yet in all the hard times, Anne
could still love and praise God.

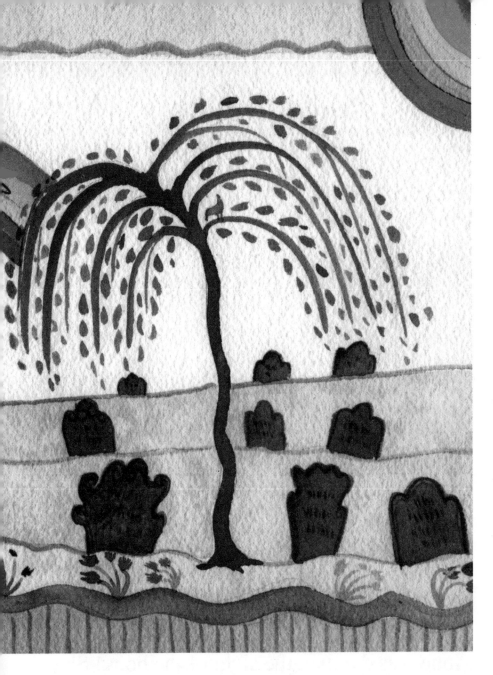

One day a book came that had Anne's name on it! It was full of Anne's poems, and it came from a printing shop in England!

Anne was dumb at the sight of the book! She had never thought of printing her poems. She thought some were too coarse to be in a book. She wrote them out one more time so they would be right.

Today you can find Anne Bradstreet's book of poems and read them yourself. You will see what a wise and true saint she was.

Now you know Anne Bradstreet.